This is

She's about to go on one of her many

adventures

in Whimsy Wood....

The Whimsy Wood Series

Posie Pixie
and the
Copper Kettle

By
Sarah Hill

Illustrations By
Sarah Mauchline

Published by:
Abela Publishing
Sandhurst, England
[2013]

Posie Pixie and the Copper Kettle

Copyright © SARAH HILL 2013

All rights reserved. No part of this book may be reproduced in any manner in any media, or transmitted by any means whatsoever, electronic, electrostatic, magnetic tape, or mechanical (including photocopy, file or video recording, internet web sites, blogs, wikis, or any other information storage and retrieval system) without the prior written permission of the publisher or author.

Published in England
by
Abela Publishing Ltd.
Sandhurst, Berkshire, England

ISBN 13: 978-1-909302-20-4

Email Posie at
posie@abelapublishing.com

Website:
www.abelapublishing.com/copper-kettle.html

First Edition 2013

10% of the net profits from this book will be donated to
THE WILDLIFE TRUSTS

Thank you to all those who have helped make

my ' Whimsy Wood ' dream become a reality

For my Grandma Phyllis

POSIE PIXIE
AND
THE COPPER KETTLE

"Oh pips and petals! Where am I going to live?" muttered Posie Pixie in a fluster, as she hurried through Whimsy Wood one warm August afternoon.

Her little bluebell hat jingled and tinkled as she bobbed up and down and scurried like a squirrel amongst the pink and purple foxgloves. " Summer's coming to an end and I must find a new home for the autumn ! " she said, looking at the woodland flowers that had started to lose their petals.

Posie was feeling a little hot and bothered now with all her hurrying and scurrying, so she stopped and leant against a large tree stump to catch her breath and cool down a bit.

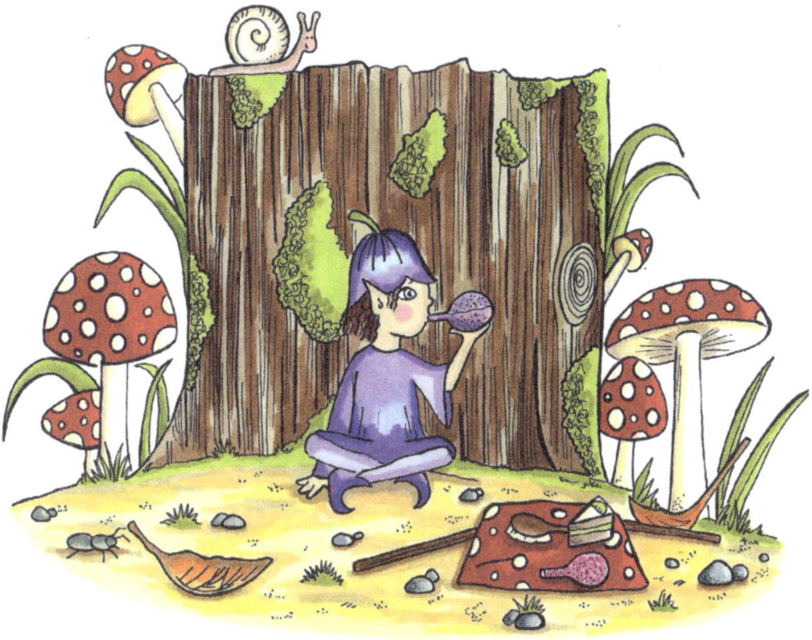

She wiped her brow and untied the red and white polka-dot handkerchief that was holding her belongings onto the little hazel twig she'd been carrying. Inside the handkerchief were two sparkly pixie bottles of strawberry lemonade, a large slice of apple cake and her hawthorn hairbrush.

Posie sat down by the tree stump and took a sip of the scrummy strawberry lemonade. As she sipped, she thought about her summer; " I've had a brilliant time with Bristle Bumblebee and Dewberry Dragonfly. We played hide and seek amongst the pretty meadow flowers nearby, danced around the daisies and slid down the high hollyhocks," she said to herself smiling.

" My pretty home in the poppies was lots of fun to live in, but it's lost all its scarlet shady petals now! With autumn on its way, I must find a home where I'll be cosy and dry."

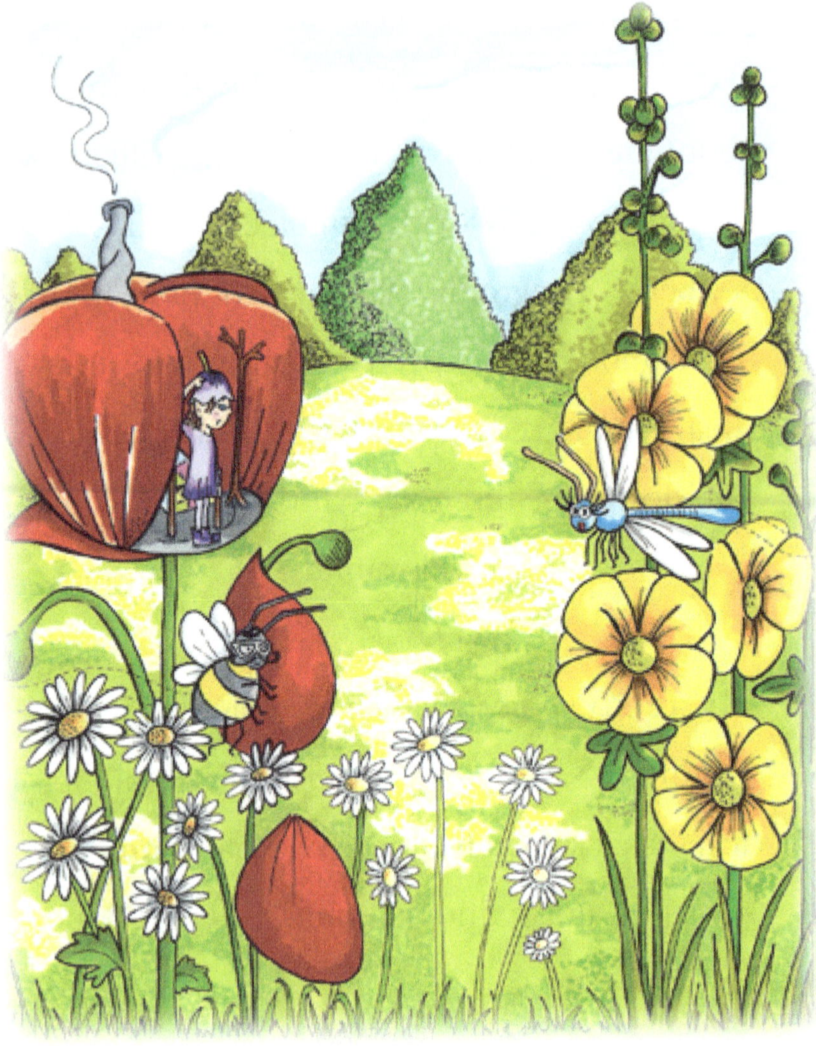

Before she could think anymore , Posie was surprised by a strange clanging and banging sound getting louder and louder behind her .

She turned around to see a beautiful sky-blue caravan being pulled through the wood by a large brown and white carthorse. A round cheerful woman with rosy red cheeks and dark curly hair was sitting at the front of the caravan. She was holding onto the horse's reins and singing a merry song as they rode along.

*"Fiddle-dee-dum and fiddle-dee-dee,
I'm as happy as I can be!
Trotting along with Henry horse,
For I am Rosa-May of course!"*

Now being quite a shy pixie, Posie darted behind the tree stump to hide. From there, she could see the caravan swaying

to and fro, to and fro; its bright shiny copper pots and pans swinging and clanging as it went.

Just as the horse reached Posie's tree stump , he whinnied and lifted one of his hooves . . . . .

The caravan wobbled from side to side and the copper pots and pans crashed loudly together . Some of them fell clattering to the ground and bounced off the gnarled and knobbly tree roots on the woodland floor .

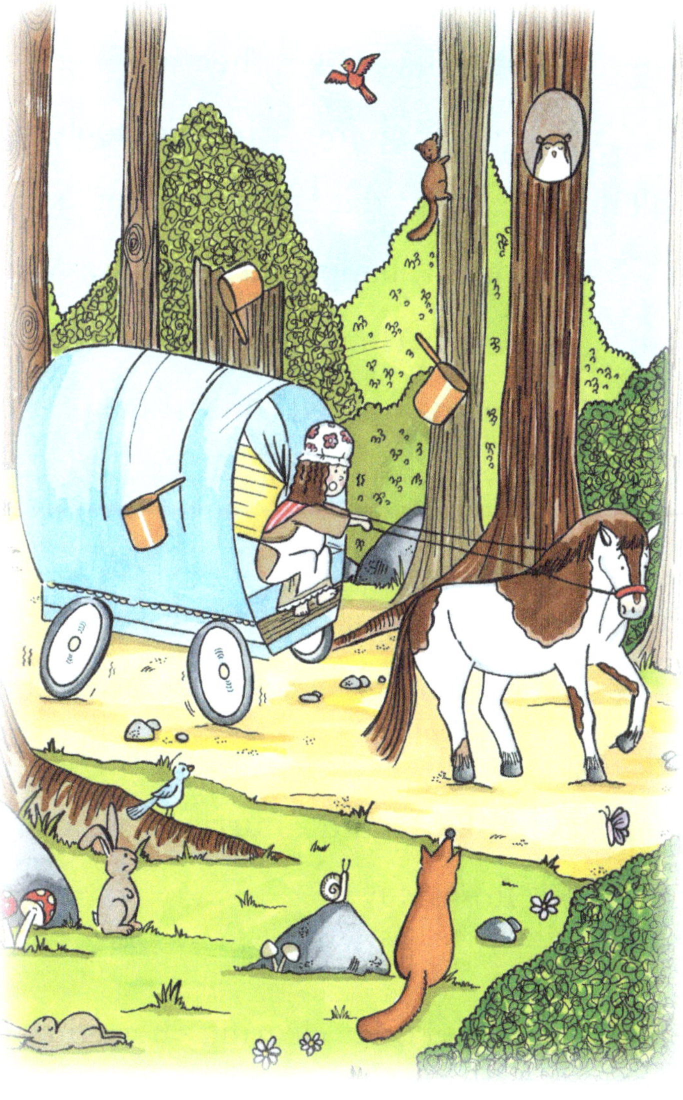

" Henry me old flower, what's the matter?" asked Rosa-May rather alarmed.

" It's no good going ' hobble-hobble, hobble-hobble ' like dat! We'd better stop and see what's happened. " Rosa-May pulled gently on Henry's reins to steady him and then clambered down from the caravan.

Although Posie was a shy pixie, she was also very kind and loved to help. Feeling much braver, she came out from behind her hiding place and hurried over to Henry and Rosa-May.

" Ahem! " said Posie clearing her throat and brushing down her purple tunic.

" Hello there . I'm Posie Pixie , " she said brightly as she adjusted her jingling tinkling bluebell hat .

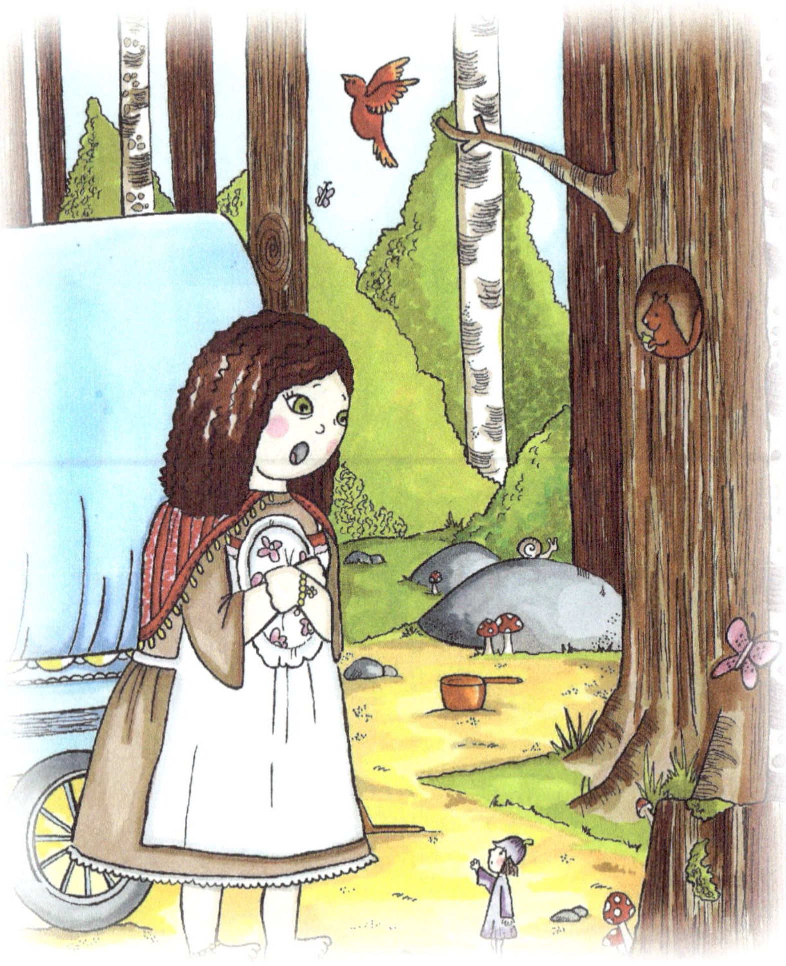

"You seem to be in a spot of bother. Can I help you and your huge horse?"

" J-J-Jumping junipers ! " said Rosa-May stepping backwards and clutching her flowery cloth-cap . Then she rubbed her eyes and said , " Bless me eyes and tickle me chin with a thistle ! A pixie ! I've not seen one of ya charming little treasures in ages ! It's a pleasure ta meet ya ta be sure ! Dis is me big brave horse Henry and I'm Rosa-May don't ya know ! If ya can help us , I'd be most grateful . "

" Well , I met some similar cheery folk to yourself in a meadow nearby a while ago . They were very friendly and full of song!

They also seemed to be very wise , as they taught me that dock leaves make a sting from a stinging nettle go away , if you rub it where you've been stung of course and that bluebells make great pixie hats! So it'd be a pleasure to help you!" replied Posie smiling and feeling very important. "If you could lift Henry's hoof up please then I'll see what I can do."

"Right ya are," said Rosa-May. "Come on Henry me boy! Up up!" she said lifting Henry's hoof. Posie could see a large spiky thorn sticking out from underneath his dinner-plate sized hoof.

"Aaah ha! I see what the problem is!" said Posie and quick as a flash she pulled the sharp thorn out.

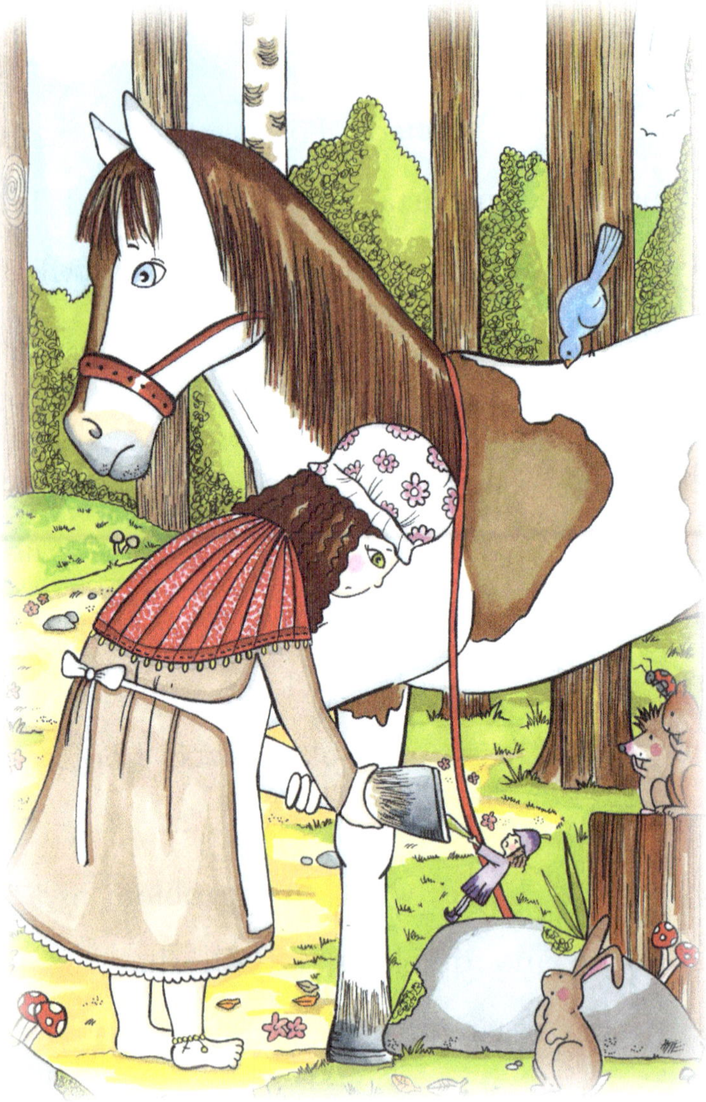

The huge horse shook his head and mane with relief , neighing gratefully as he did so . His hoof wasn't sore anymore and he could stand comfortably on it .

" There there Henry you brave chap , " said Posie kindly whilst stroking his fluffy brown and white leg .
" You're as good as new ! "

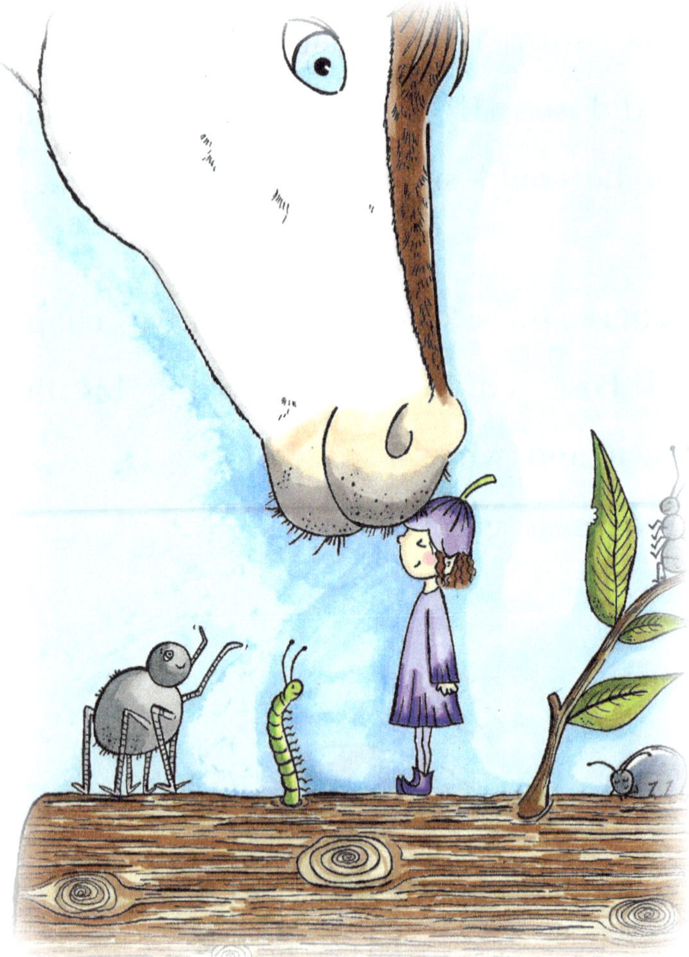

Henry bent his head down low and rubbed his nose gently on top of Posie's bluebell hat in a friendly fashion. This made Posie giggle!

"Well now, dat's just marvellous!" said Rosa-May chuckling and clapping her ringed hands together in delight. "T'ank ya muchly for helping us. I don't know what I'd do without my Henry! He's me best friend," she said patting his strong shoulder.

"He pulls me caravan wherever we go and keeps me company all the while. I'm much obliged ta ya for pulling out that naughty thorn and making Henry's sore hoof better. In return for ya kindness, ya can choose one of me special copper pots and pans dat've fallen to the ground as we root around for dem. Ya can keep it if yu'd like."

Posie was thrilled and did a little pixie dance! Her purple pointy pixie boots darted about so quickly that Rosa-May had to rub her eyes again to see them! Then she scurried about the woodland floor looking this way and that for the shiny pots and pans, so Rosa-May could put them back onto her caravan.

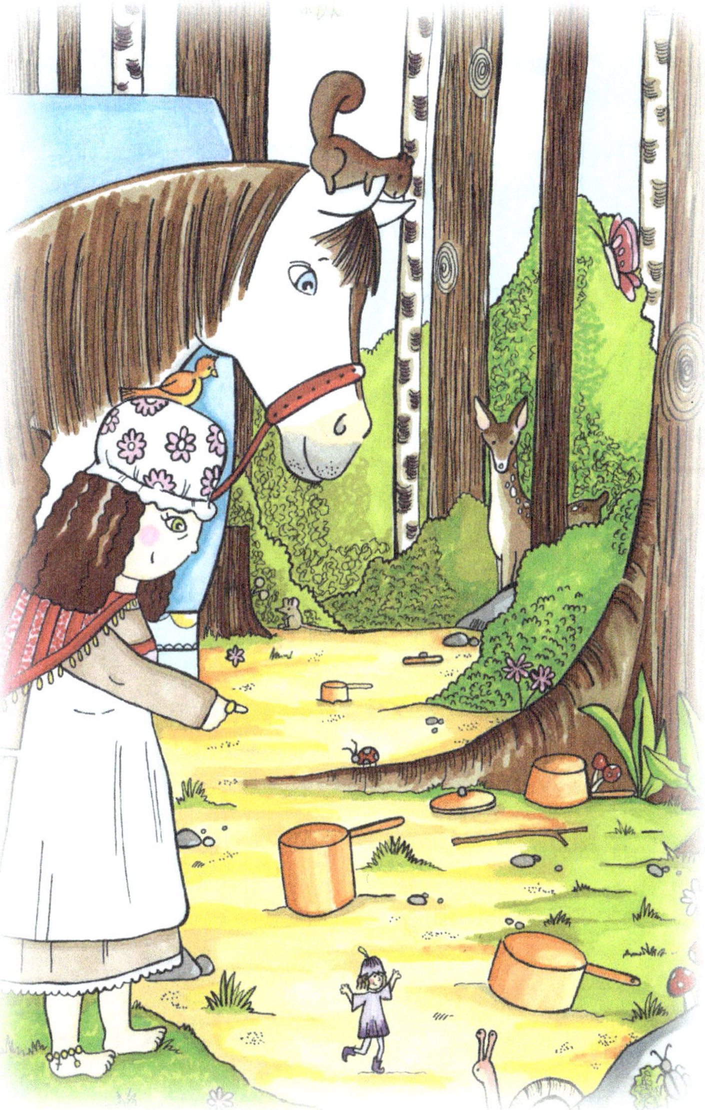

Finally she chose a rather unusual copper kettle to keep for herself. It was bigger than the others and now had a few dents in it from its fall.

"I'd love to keep this quirky copper kettle please," she said to Rosa-May and pointed to a rather peculiar shaped kettle that was lying on its side by a tree root.

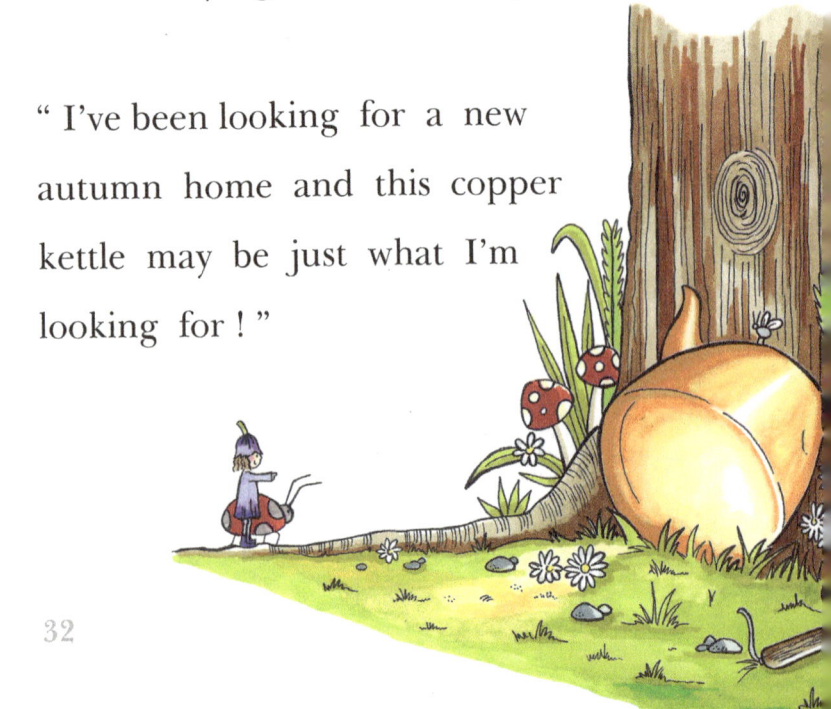

"I've been looking for a new autumn home and this copper kettle may be just what I'm looking for!"

"Aaah yes. Dat smashing kettle's a grand choice ta be sure. It's brought me good luck on me travels and always made a cracking cup of cha. I'm sure it'll make a fine home for a fine pixie!" she said winking at Posie. "Now where shall we be putting it?"

"Over there please," said Posie pointing towards the tree stump she'd been hiding behind and where she'd left her belongings to help Henry.

"Aaah, I like ya thinking! Yu'll be nicely sheltered there," she replied and with that, she placed Posie's new shiny home up against the tree stump. Then she put a few stones on either side of the kettle to keep it secure on the woodland floor.

"Look 'ere!" said Rosa-May pointing to the stones she'd placed near the kettle's side that had the spout.

"When ya climb dese stones, ya can use the spout to slide into ya new home!"

" Wow ! That's a brilliant idea ! " squeaked Posie as she jumped up and down with delight , which made her bluebell hat jingle and tinkle . " I love sliding ! It's sooo much fun ! "

" Come round dis side Posie , " said Rosa-May beckoning with her finger , as she crouched down to look at the copper kettle's handle . " Dere's now a hole in the kettle's side where the handle was attached . It must've come away when it fell ta the ground . Ya could use dis hole as a doorway . "
" Yes I certainly could ! " said Posie , hopping excitedly from foot to foot . " There's some little hooks by the hole

too , which I guess helped keep the handle in place . If we hook a large leaf onto these then I'll have a door " she said, pointing up at the tiny hooks .

" Well would ya look at dat ! I'm a lucky lady today alright ! " exclaimed Rosa-May , whilst flapping her white frilly apron up and down . " I've found ya leaf door ! " she said and bent down to pick a shiny green dock leaf . Then she helped Posie hang her new dock leaf front door .

" Dere now . All done , " said Rosa-May smiling as she stood up and rearranged her lacey petticoats .

" That's wonderful ! " Posie said happily and she smiled back up at Rosa-May . " Thank you for my perfect new autumn home ! " she said and with that , she curtsied and shook Rosa-May's finger . "

" Dat's a pleasure me dear ! " replied Rosa-May curtsying in return . " It's the

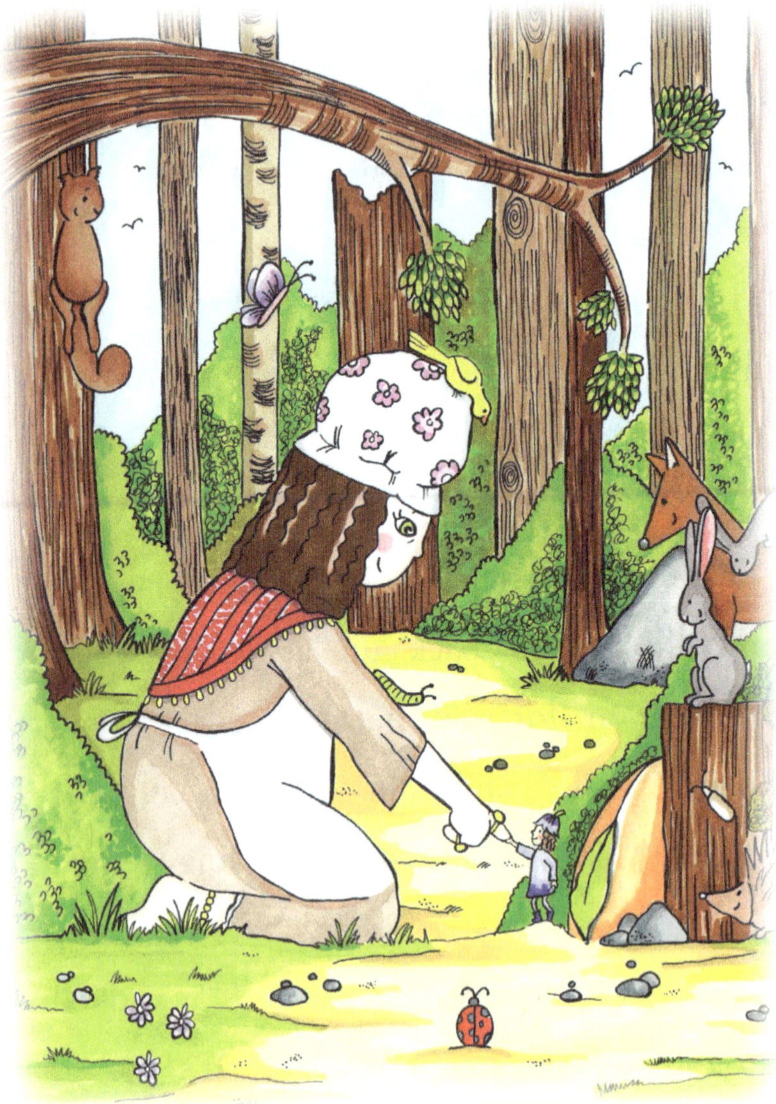

least I could do and besides Posie, as me wise old Granny used to say, 'One good turn always deserves another'."

"Oooh I like that! I'll try and remember it!" said Posie, smiling and waving as Rosa-May clambered back up onto her sky-blue caravan.

"Well now, enough of this blathering! We should be getting on our way. Come on Henry me boy," said Rosa-May shaking his reins. Henry snorted and winked at Posie, before he trotted off happily pulling Rosa-May and her beautiful sky-blue caravan.

Posie giggled to herself and then turned to admire her shiny new copper kettle house with its dock leaf front door and spout slide.

The Whimsy Wood series

Enter a world of enchantment and wonder. See more of Posie Pixie by searching for

"Whimsy Wood"

on

FACEBOOK

The Whimsy Wood Series

By
SARAH HILL

Illustrated by
SARAH MAUCHLINE

Look out for Posie's next adventure in

Book 2

Posie Pixie

and

The Lost Matchbox

AUTHOR'S BIO

' Sarah Hill is a small animal Vet. She gained her Veterinary Medicine degree at Bristol University in 1999 and worked in practice for 10 years. At that point she had her second daughter and soon after she decided to take a career break. She now writes her children's series, 'Whimsy Wood', at home in Wiltshire with her husband, two daughters, two dogs, two cats and " a partridge in a pear tree " ! They are currently expecting their third child...... '

ILLUSTRATOR'S BIO

' Sarah Mauchline has been illustrating from a young age and it has always been her passion. She has illustrated for both childrens' books and for the crafting industry. Her three young children are an inspiration when it comes to drawing and she will always seek their approval upon completion of an illustration. Her style is fun, colourful and unique which compliments the wonderfully creative Whimsy Wood literature.'

Published by

www.AbelaPublishing.com